The
Creeks

An Upland Adventure

This Was Anneca.

The
Creeks

an upland adventure

by
Craig Kulchak
Photographs by the Author

The Walkabout Press Company · Boise, Idaho
Copy Right © 1996 by
Craig and Lisa Kulchak

Edited by
Laura Brunson

ISBN 0-9655833-0-9
Library of Congress
Catalog Card Number 96-90968

Printed in the United States of America

To Lisa, Kip, Matt and Nate ~
my Wife and Sons.

Contents

Introduction

This book first started as just a means of keeping track of my day to day bird hunting trips with my two setters Anneca and Beth. One day after going through some of my shooting diary notes, I came up with the idea of taking some of the better hunts and compiling them into some sort of book form. I'd work on transferring my shooting diary notes into more readable text after work, or on the weekends but nothing on a full time schedule. Then about three years ago I was close enough to start the process of the book design and just how many of my stories would be included. With a little help from Trent Hill, a friend of mine, to get my creative juices flowing and some encouragement from my wife Lisa, things just fell into place.

I've separated The Creeks into two parts. The first, *Far and Away*, deals with hunts that required lengthy travel and, for the most part, camping over night. The second, *Close to Home*, deals with hunts that were pretty much an hour from town. The final chapter, When, is the last real hunt that Anneca, Beth and I had together; after which we mostly spent our time chasing preserve released pheasants.

The Creeks wasn't written to make some sort of profound statement or introduce some new method of hunting. It seems that the people that hunt or fish just have this need to share their experiences with others of their kind and, I'm afraid, I'm no different. So find that favorite wing back chair or that over stuffed couch, set aside a few hours and let me take you with me and my setters on a few hunts for grouse, chukar and quail in my state of Idaho.

Part One: Far and Away

The Creeks

Two-Bit
Creek

Perfection.

Two-bit Creek

There comes a time in an upland hunter's life when he stumbles upon an area that surpasses all the other places he has been fortunate enough to hunt. Two-Bit Creek was just such a place. It was the fall of 1982 when Keith Bloom, an old high school and college buddy, and I first discovered this creek. Despite its name it was worth its weight in gold. Over the years I have saved this area for the opening weekend of grouse season only and I do not hunt it any other time.

The first time an area is hunted is always the most special - unknowns around each bend, the ultimate sense of exploration and adventure. My entry for the creek's maiden hunt in my shooting diary was all of these things and more:

Keith Bloom and I left for the mountains along the South Fork of the Salmon River this afternoon after work. I had spent the night before gathering up gear, cleaning my gun, and talking to Anneca and Beth about our plans for the weekend. I could tell they knew there was adventure ahead. They both sat in silence as I talked, staring into the darkness of the evening, listening to my every word.

The drive up was an adventure in itself. With daylight fading we followed the banks of the Payette River through canyons of aspen and pine. Keith talked of his time overseas working in Saudi Arabia and of his trips to the Orient. He talked, I listened, watching the canyon turn from a pink- yellow to a deep purple as the sun fell behind the horizon.

It was dark when we rolled into Cascade, the final stop to gas up before the last hour of our drive into camp. Keith drank the better part of a half-gallon of wine as we drove and though he had talked the whole way, he now sat in quiet contemplation for the drive into camp.

It had rained all week and the weekend forecast called for more of the same. But with the higher elevations of the surrounding area, Keith and I gambled on missing the rain. A misty fog followed us up to the summit, then disappeared as we made our decent into the valley below. We left the main road and turned off to camp, the tires of the van splashing through rain puddles left from the passing storm as if telegraphing our arrival. Another ten minutes and we were in camp.

With the night air biting at our fingers and noses the first order of business was to start a fire. Just to be on the safe side, Keith had talked me into bringing a reserve of split pine in case of wet conditions. It was a suggestion I had fought from the beginning and in Keith's condition he was not about to let me forget.

The mountain air was crisp and held the threat of frost, but the fire made the night air bearable. As we sat in its warm glow watching the flames dance before us, a large crack from the center of the fire brought us back to reality. It was time to set up the tent. Keith was adamant about helping with the tent poles but with one quick stroll through the fire and a shoulder roll out the other side that ended in a cloud of dust, he convinced me it was time to designate him chief supervisor of tent pole construction. He spent the rest of the night sitting in a director's chair giving incoherent instructions on the proper method of tent pole installation. I let Keith rest while I unloaded the rest of the gear into the tent. By convincing him I'd be chipping him out of his chair in the morning with an ice pick if he stayed, I coaxed him into the tent.

Morning came quickly. Keith rose from his slumber as if nothing had taken place the night before (a gift he has always been blessed with), stretched, yawned and with a smile said, "Lets eat." Clanking around the camp supplies like an old bear just out of hibernation, he wrestled the cast iron frying pan from the bottom of the supply box, lit the camp stove and started cooking breakfast. We were excited about the day's hunt, but breakfast assumed a leisurely pace. After the clean-up from breakfast we loaded up the dogs and drove to the base of two creeks that emptied into the south fork of the Salmon River. We stopped at the first creek and got out for a look around. The terrain was steep. Keith suggested the area could be better hunted if we split up. So, with the traditional flip of a coin, Kieth chose the right side of the creek.

I stood and watched as Keith and his dog, Ben, disappeared into the trees, waited a few minutes, then cast Anneca and Beth up the steep grade toward a dense group of chokecherries. The weather was perfect. The cover looked promising and when Beth's bell went silent I knew all the planning had paid off. It took five minutes before I located Beth. I came to a clearing and on the slope above it was Beth...rock solid! I walked in for the flush. No bird. Beth moved ahead to relocate but nothing came of it. I stopped to rethink the situation. Then I spotted a grouse perched in the lower branches of a fir tree, stretching out its neck, trying to hide among the bows.

Beth hadn't seen the bird and I called her to me in hopes that she'd spot it. Grabbing her by the collar, I pointed to the bird. She went solid. By this time Anneca, hearing my call, arrived. This was too much for the bird. Within seconds of Anneca's arrival, it exploded from the tree. The grouse flushed into a clearing that offered

This was Keith

an unusually open shot. I took the bird at about thirty yards, folding it in a cloud of feathers. The thick cover made finding the grouse difficult for Anneca but after a short search, she found it and retrieved it beautifully. With the first grouse of the day lying heavy in my game pouch, we stopped to shortly rest before climbing higher.

As we reflected on the events that had just unfolded, a shot echoed from across the valley telling me that Keith and Ben had just scored on their first grouse of the day as well. It was time to move on.

We took one last drink from the canteen then traversed the steep grade to the top of the ridge above. The next half-hour passed without encountering a single grouse. The sun was breaking through the clouds, causing steam to rise from the dense cover. It was a welcome sight. Anneca, Beth and I found an open space, and took time to warm ourselves in the sun's glow. I heard another shot, then decided to hunt in the direction of the van. Turning toward the location of the last shot, I grabbed the girls by their collars and cast them downhill.

The rain from the night before made walking difficult. I found myself using the branches from small trees like a mountain climber uses a rope to repel from a cliff. We came to a small clearing with Beth flash pointing then moving ahead to relocate. As Anneca came into the same area, she locked on point. I tried to send her on but she wouldn't budge. Moving closer, I could see Beth on point about 15 yards downhill from Anneca. She was at the base of a fir with branches that reached to the ground. I moved a few more steps closer. Anneca moved ahead only to lock up solidly once more. I was less than ten feet behind Beth when I heard small peeping sounds ahead of her. As I moved closer, Beth's head began slowly moving to her right. The birds were moving.

I took another step and grouse started flushing from behind the fir - one, two and three at a time. I perpaired for the next brace of birds as I took the first one just before it disappeared behind a dense fir, then the second as it reappeared from behind the same tree. This was my second lifetime double on grouse and I was elated. Anneca broke and moved to retrieve while Beth held her ground until the last grouse had flushed, then ran to help Anneca locate the fallen birds. As Anneca brought the first bird to hand, Beth, who didn't like the feel of something dead in her jowls, stayed to mark the second. Two beautiful points, three shots and three grouse; it couldn't get any better.

After a short break, we followed the line of flight taken by the last grouse flushed. Each step became tougher as we made our way through the thick cover and steep grade. The wet conditions from   last night's storm made the footing treacherous. We walked for another 20 minutes, then came to a small pocket where the headwaters of the creeks began. There were dead falls all around. Although it took some maneuvering, we welcomed the lack of thick cover.

Anneca and Beth were out in front some 50 yards. Although I couldn't see the dogs in the dense cover, I could hear their bells harmonizing as they worked the plateau below me. The bell duet suddenly turned solo. I knew one had pinned down another grouse somewhere ahead. Moving in the direction of where I had last heard the bell, I rounded a large fir. There at its base I found Beth, rock solid, staring up into the tree's branches. Anneca was working a small patch of chokecherry above me when she spotted Beth pointing and froze to back. I stopped to take a few photos of the point, then moved in for the flush.

As I drew closer to Beth, I followed her line of sight and could see the grouse peering down at her. Two more steps and the bird spotted me. Its crest erect, it positioned itself for flight.

I looked down for a better spot to stand when the lower branches of the tree exploded. The grouse made its escape. Fumbling for the gun's safety, I pulled off two shots. The bird faltered then fluttered to the ground with the second. I could hear the dying wingbeats of the grouse on the forest floor as Beth and Anneca headed in to retrieve. Anneca's position above the grouse had given her a better view and she was on the bird in no time. Beth was still searching 20 yards ahead of me when the sound of two more flushes came from the group of chokecherries Anneca had been working before the first flush. Then I realized that the back I had thought Anneca had made on Beth's point was actually her point on the two departing grouse.

Off in the distance I could hear the slow tinkling of Anneca's bell coming closer, a sound that signaled she was coming with her bird. Calling Beth in, I waited for Anneca to deliver the last grouse of the day. Anneca had trouble navigating through the group of dead falls below, but soon laid the grouse at my feet, a young Franklin male. We sat on a large fallen log in the middle of a small clearing and broke for lunch, the four grouse lined up in a row on my left, Anneca and Beth on my right. Both had silly grins that reflected a day's work well done. Finished with lunch, we headed back to the van. Keith and Ben had worked their way to the top of the canyon's opposite side so it was some time before he and Ben rejoined us. Keith had had bagged one female Franklin grouse with the two shots I had heard earlier that morning. He had seen a few large blue grouse near the top of the canyon, but had been unable to shoot in the thick cover. By the time Keith and Ben returned to the van, it was late afternoon. With five grouse to our credit, we headed back to camp to start dinner and fish a little in Warm Lake.

We pulled into camp at five o'clock, cleaned the birds, plopped three into a large Dutch oven with a few carrots, potatoes and spices, turned the camp stove on low and headed for the lake. While we tried for small brookies and rainbows, Anneca, Beth and Ben cooled themselves in the icy lake.

We spent an hour fishing small dries in hopes of a trout break-fast. Though unsuccessful, we welcomed the break in the action from the day's hunt.

As we approached camp, the smell of roast grouse greeted us. We spent the rest of that evening around the fire reliving the day's events, listening to the sounds of the night and preparing for tomorrow's hunt.

Beth with our four grouse.

Six-Bit Creek

This is what Six - Bit was all about.

Six-Bit
Creek

September 01, 1983:

Back at the Dollar Creeks. It was like coming home. Paul Dougherty was my hunting partner this season. Paul and I had both worked together in Alaska this summer and shared a study room in college. He bought Mel, a chocolate lab, last spring and brought her along for her first grouse work. She was a beautiful dog with a mild temperament, a great nose and excellent retrieving skills. Paul was hoping for a hunt as successful as last season's and some fantastic dog work.

The weather was cooperating, overcast with a light drizzle. We pulled into camp just before dusk and had time to set up the tent with natural light. Keith Bloom was on my mind as we set the tent poles. He was in Maryland this fall. I would miss both his company and antics. I welcomed Paul's help with the tent; my thoughts turned to Keith's 'help' last year. We made a dinner of this year's early season deer steaks, peppers, new potatoes and fresh mushrooms, simmered the Dutch oven.

As dinner warmed our bellies, we turned in for the night. Beth and Anneca were like a couple of kids with Christmas Eve jitters; they both knew where we were and why we were here. Morning came with the chattering of a family of mountain jays raiding the scraps from last night's dinner, left on the camp table. Their raid was short lived thanks to Mel. Breakfast was quick, bagels and cream cheese with orange juice to wash it down. After breakfast, we packed lunches, loaded up the girls and headed out to the Dollar Creeks. We drove past Two-Bit Creek and headed for the canyon ridge by the headwaters of Six-Bit.

The road up seemed worse than I had remembered. In several places the spring run off washed large ruts, making the slow drive up seem even slower. When we reached the summit, we pulled off to the side of the trail and parked. We had a choice; we could hunt north or south across the ridge. The cover looked better and the going easier to the north, so we started there. Last night's rain made walking rough. I had to keep one eye on the dogs ahead, the other for any branches lying in wait to send me crashing to the ground. The further we went, the steeper the slope became. Finally, a wooden assassin leapt out between my boot heel and sole and sent me to the forest floor, bending the ventilated rib on my gun.

Anneca and Beth were 40 yards downhill ahead of me while Mel, unsure of the dense cover, walked at Paul's heel the whole morning. Beth was working above in a stand of young fir while Anneca covered the ground below. Beth had that birdy gait so, nursing my hip from the fall, I hurried to close the distance between us. At about 20 yards Anneca ran into the middle of a group of 15 Franklin grouse. A brace folded at the bark of my Harrington Richardson; the rest scattered into the trees and surrounding brush.

Beth was walking up to every tree and looking into the branches above; she knew where the birds were! Paul started in my direction and I called to him to let him know there were still birds in the area.

He was 20 yards behind me when a brace flushed from his right. The first shot dropped one in a cloud of feathers, the second shot missed as the grouse sailed into the valley below. Mel was moving in to retrieve the first grouse when another flushed from the branches above Paul. He held his shot until the bird was about 25 yards out. Paul centered the grouse and it hit the ground with a thump, rolling and fluttering down the steep grade of the mountain side.

Anneca moved downhill to retrieve as feathers cascaded to the ground. She delivered to hand and as we stood beneath the trees, we could hear the calls of more grouse above us. Every so often one of the birds would lose its nerve, flush from the safety of the trees and with wings cupped, sail into the canyon below. With four birds to our credit, we left the area and headed south to another promising patch of cover.

The walking was easier and the trees and chokecherries were spread out a bit more, all of which would allow clear shots if we got into more grouse. We had covered some 200 yards without moving a single bird. The ridge we were walking turned to the right. Traveling a few more yards, I came across a trickle of a creek that cut its way through dead falls, forming a small basin harboring patches of chokecherry and huckelberry. Anneca and Beth were working cover to my left; Beth about 30 yards ahead, Anneca 25 yards uphill. Paul and Mel were below me, some sixty yards from the basin.

As we came to the edge of the basin, five grouse flushed in front of Anneca. She gave a short chase, came back with that silly grin of hers to apologize for the lapse in concentration, then spun around and started working promising cover to my right, as if nothing had happened. Within a few yards she was on a bird, her tail traveling in circles as she moved in slow motion. Moving ahead, I spotted the grouse on the ground. It was heading in Anneca's direction, but then disappeared into a dense patch of brush next to a large deadfall. Anneca went solid, pointing in a low crouching position. While I moved to her side, I could see her head turn and slowly angle to the left. The bird was moving.

Walking in quickly, I started kicking the brush around the deadfall. The grouse shot out from under my feet, sending a shower of leaves trailing behind it as it flew downhill in Paul's direction. "Bird your way," I shouted. Paul waved to let me know he was ready. At 30 yards the grouse spotted him and flared uphill into a dense group of fir. Anneca, Beth and I followed while Paul and Mel moved to the logging road below in case the grouse headed for the canyon.

The girls and I were 15 yards from the stand of fir when the bird exploded from the upper branches, heading uphill. I took my first shot at around 20 yards, missing cleanly. The shot turned the grouse and it flew straight away. At 30 yards my second shot dropped the bird clean. Anneca retrieved to hand. With a pat on her side and a 'good girl,' I placed the grouse in my game pouch, then headed toward Paul who was waiting for us with Mel on the logging road somewhere below.

Paul couldn't see me when I made my second shot, but saw the grouse fold and Anneca make the recovery and disappear into the brush. We all sat beside the logging road for a short break and planned the next route back to the van. The clouds were breaking up and we welcomed the warm rays of the sun cutting through the overcast sky.

We planned to take the most direct route to the van - the logging road. There was considerable ground we had not covered. There was a good chance the dogs would make game as we traveled up the road. We hadn't gone far when Beth went on point below a group of elderberries that jutted from the edge of the washed out slope on the right side of the road. Anneca was ten yards behind Beth, spotted her on point, then moved in to honor. Paul and I walked in quickly for the flush, carrying our guns at port of arms. As we drew closer, the birds became nervous and started moving uphill. By this time, Mel had caught up with Anneca and Beth. She made scent of the grouse and moved up the slope, stepped in front of Beth and jumped right into the middle of the birds. Ready, I had a clear shot as the grouse headed for the thicker cover above and managed to drop a single. Paul had been standing behind me and was unable to shoot. The rest of the grouse scattered among the trees above. As I had already made my limit for the day, I let Paul work the remaining grouse alone.

At the shot, Beth had broke point and rushed uphill to locate the downed birds as Anneca and Mel followed. With Beth's distaste for anything deceased, she let Anneca and Mel retrieve and headed to Paul to locate living game. As she past Paul, she moved to his right and traversed the slope in a straight line for about 20 yards before she located another grouse in the lower branches of a small fir. She locked up solid and waited for Paul to move in for the flush. As he drew closer, the bird spotted Paul and with crest erect, readied for escape. Paul took another step and the grouse flushed in a clap of wings, heading for a dense stand of fir 15 yards straight away. He managed to shoot just as the grouse made the stand of fir, but was unsure of whether or not he had connected. We searched the area thoroughly, but came up with nothing. Reluctantly, we headed back to the van.

We returned to camp in time to fish before preparing the day's grouse for dinner. Fishing from the bank as the sun began to set, the excitement from the afternoon's hunt was behind us as the silence of the lakeside overtook us. Anneca, Beth and Mel sat by our sides while we tried our luck with small surface flies and tiny nymphs in the surface film of the lake on what seemed to be nonexistent fish. Fishing after the first day's hunt with no luck was becoming a tradition. My thoughts turned to last year's trip with Keith Bloom and his Golden Retriever Ben. In their memory, I cut short the fishing. No sense of ruining a tradition by catching something. Paul agreed, and after breaking down our fly fishing gear, we headed up the trail back to camp.

Paul set up the camp stove while I prepared two of the largest grouse for dinner. In a paper bag I mixed salt, pepper and some rye flour, placed the birds in the bag, coating each grouse with the mixture. Meanwhile, Paul cut up carrots, celery and new russet potatoes and sauteed them in virgin olive oil in the Dutch oven. After dinner we sat around the campfire, cleaned our guns and relived the success of the day's hunt.

We slept in the next morning, waking to overcast skies and a slight drizzle. We took breakfast in the warmth of the tent while we planed for a quick hunt before heading home. We broke camp and headed for the creeks, arriving at Six-Bit around 11 o'clock. The first draw we hunted looked promising, but produced nothing. As we came back to the van, the rain picked up. Paul was anxious to leave, but I convinced him to stay so we could try one more ridge before heading home.

I cast the girls across the road up the ridge opposite the van while Paul, who had had enough of the rain, sat in the van with Mel. The ground cover was tight, low-lying huckelberry with a few chokecherry bushes and fir trees scattered about. To the left was the road heading back to camp, its length edged with dogwood. Beth and Anneca hadn't gone far when both bells went silent. I rounded the edge of a thick stand of chokecherry and spotted Anneca on point. A few more steps and I could see Beth ahead on point. Ten yards in front of her was a large Franklin male. I moved slowly forward and immediately the grouse flushed. I shot through the thick cover and saw the bird fall on the other side of a deadfall. Beth broke with Anneca right behind her. Both disappeared into the surrounding cover. When I reached the deadfall, Beth was standing over the grouse, growling. This was her bird. Although she wasn't keen about picking up the grouse, Beth was not about to let Anneca share the glory of the retrieve. I patted her side and picked the grouse up, holding it above Anneca and Beth as they buried their noses in its feathers, drinking in the sweet scent that makes their souls burn.

This was a perfect end to opening weekend of the season. I decided not to push my luck. Back at the van, I lifted up the grouse to show Paul our success. He smiled and gave a thumbs up, acknowledging my good luck. We spent the next three hours driving back home, talking of other hunting trips and planning next year's trip to the Dollar Creeks.

Anneca, Beth and the Author ~
a perfect end.

The Creeks

The Big Lost

The Big Lost ~
vast and lonely.

The
Big Lost

There is urgency in the fall. It is a time of changing leaves, shorter days and colder nights. It's a feeling that comes over me that I have a hard time explaining, as if Father Time is telling me to do it now or it's lost forever. With every hunting season that passes, there is always one trip when this feeling overcomes me, causing me to break down and answer its beckoning call.

It was the fall of 1986 when I discovered The Big Lost. I had been promising myself for the past six years to take a weekend and hunt the short sage hen season. Because of the distances I needed to travel and any other excuse I could come up with, I hadn't taken the time. My shooting diary shows this year to be different:

September 20, 1986: Took Anneca and Beth sage hen hunting today. Weather was mild — in the low eighties. Anneca had one productive and two backs, Beth had three productives and one back. Four shots fired, with three birds downed. Anneca made all three retrieves — one from the middle of the Big Lost at the bottom of the canyon. I had to climb like a goat to get it from her.

This was the final weekend of the season for sage grouse. Gathering up gun, Anneca, Beth, gear and lunch, I loaded the van and headed for destinations unknown. The drive seemed to take forever. As we passed good looking chukar cover I kept wanting to play it safe and just go for the sure thing. But that damned Gypsy blood drove me on.

At last we pulled into Fairfield, the halfway point, and we stopped to top off the tank and stretch our legs a bit. The drive had taken its toll on Anneca and Beth and their patience was running thin. Filling their water dish, I promised them both we would be hunting soon.

The second leg of the trip took us past Magic Reservoir, the Little Wood River and famous Silver Creek. Driving through the Silver Creek area there was a full-blown hatch of Light Cahill and Blue Dun. The insects were splattering on the windshield and the grill of the van. It sounded like I was driving through a hail storm. As we crossed culvert after culvert, I wished I had my fly fishing gear along, but no time. It was mid-morning when we reached a small farm town just short of the Craters of the Moon. With daylight burning, we decided to hunt the first good looking cover.

We were three miles past the farm town when I spotted a small dirt road heading north. There was a small reservoir in the distance and what looked to be the remnants of a cattle ranch. It was 10:00 A.M. Finding a place to turn around , I quickly made the turn-off and headed for the ranch. As we rounded a corner in the road, a small forked horn mule deer crossed in front of us. . He ran beside the van for about thirty yards, then and bounced up the hill side covered with aspens and went out of sight. Beth and Anneca caught site of the deer and as their noses smeared across the driver's side glass, they watched it disappear over the rise.

I pulled on to a side road into a large grove of screaming yellow and gold aspens and followed the path into a clearing. There were several large stones placed in a circle with ashes and coals in its center. A pile of firewood, weathered gray from last winters snow and the summer sun, was neatly stacked. In between two large aspens, a pole, some six inches thick, was lashed down with rusty baling wire some seven feet off the ground. It was then I realized we were standing in the middle of an old deer hunting camp. We were treading on ancient hunting grounds, not of Native Americans, but of white men. It seemed to me a good omen. I let the girls out to stretch their legs and water up before the hunt.

The camp was at the edge of the aspen grove. Beyond its fringe the land opened up into a vast rock and sage basin for miles. I called Anneca and Beth in, put their collars and bells on, pulled my gun from its sheath, strapped on my hunting vest and cast the girls into the blue-green sage beyond. The basin was enormous. As we worked our way up a stair-stepped plateau to the north, I felt humbled and insignificant in this vast expanse of 'God's country'. I had planned a sort of hopscotch hunt from here to the Big Lost River range. I'd spend a little time here, a little time there, but this place was huge. I feared that I might spend too much time on an unproductive area and fail to connect on grouse. I picked a spot 400 yards above me and decided to work the girls to only that point, then cross over to the van and then try a new spot.

The plateau we were hunting was a large finger jetting out from the side of the basin. It was about 300 yards wide, dropping off on both sides and about 800 yards long. Anneca and Beth were covering ground like a dream, setting down a zig-zag pattern from edge to edge; each working independently but aware of each other's presence at the same time. We finally reached my stopping point, but I decided to go just one hundred yards more. It was disheartening not to have any contact with birds in what seemed to be the perfect cover. We quickly closed the distance of the last few yards and reluctantly I called the girls in for a water break before heading back to the van.

We sat and shared drinks from the canteen as I looked across the basin at cover that went on for miles, all of it beckoning me to stay and explore its secrets. I wanted to stay, but as I glanced at my watch, the nomad inside me told me to move on. It was 11:00 a.m. We had sat too long. As I stood, I could feel my legs start to stiffen. Anneca and Beth weren't ready to go either but the sun was almost directly overhead and time was running out. Patting them both on their sides, I pointed them in the direction of the van and cast them both downhill.

The steep grade made walking down easy and we moved through the sage and rocks quickly. It was 11:30 A.M. when we reached the bottom of the basin. The temperature was rising, so the girls laid in the cool shade of the van while I put my gun and hunting vest away and brought out lunch. We took a half-hour break to get our pulse back to normal as I tried to rethink my hunting strategy.

I couldn't understand why there weren't any signs of grouse in what seemed to be perfect conditions. Was I too high? Was I not high enough? Or was I hunting in the wrong location all together? A cool breeze came through the trees as if to tell me, " Hurry! Move on! You're running out of time!" With a new sense of purpose, I gathered up the girls and headed back to the main road.

We drove another two miles before it happened again; a big open basin stretching out for miles, called to me. It was a while before I was able to find a way back into it, but after a short search, was able to find a small dirt road cut into the hillside. We followed the dusty trail back in the direction of the basin. We had driven for about ten minutes, when off in the distance, I spotted a large white sign at the side of the road. Soon it was close enough to read: "This area has been poison baited for coyotes." All this time for nothing. I turned around and vowed I would not turn off the road again until we were through the Craters of the Moon National Park. It was noon.

I cursed myself all the way over the pass into Arco. When we made it over the pass, my heart sank. The country opened up across the horizon and went on for hundreds of miles in all directions. Where was I going to hunt? I was running out of time. In the distance I could see the white and cream specks of houses across the blue-green sage valley. I've been in situations like this before, so I immediately started looking for someone to ask where to hunt when we reached the city limits.

Just before the city center the Big Lost cuts through town. It's more of a creek than a river. As we passed over it, I noticed a large amount of water running from bank to bank. I made the intersection where the two highways meet just past the town's theater and turned right. As luck would have it, I spotted a gas station, sporting goods store with deer and elk trophies hanging on the walls inside, staring out the window at the traffic. I topped off the tank once more and stepped inside, desperate to talk to someone about sage grouse in the area.

"Excuse me," I said. "Do you know of any good spots for sage hen around here?" The attendant looked very surprised that I had asked and was eager to help.

"Sure," he answered. "Just drive east of town and you'll see a turn off about a half mile out to the right. There's a trailer on the left hand side. If ya go across the rail road tracks, you've gone too far. Ya need to hunt along the river."

I thanked him for his help and headed for the turn off. The half mile was more like two, but we found it anyway. We made the turn off and pulled into the driveway of the trailer to ask permission to hunt and directions to the 'river'. I got out and knocked on the door but there was no answer. I knocked again and heard some shuffling from inside, but still no one. One more round of knocks brought a round and unshaven man in his late sixties to the door. He looked like he had slept in his clothes and smelled of beer, but to my surprise, was very friendly. I told him my needs and he looked at me as if I were crazy to want to hunt sage grouse. He then told me he had "seen a covey of Huns in the stubble field out behind the house this morning. They're probably still there too," he said enthusiasticlly.

I thanked him for his hospitality, but told him I needed to find the river.

"Jus' keep on this road and stay to yer left," he said. "If ya cross any gates, make sure ya close 'em. Ya know it's all right if ya shoot some of them Huns."

I thanked him once more and headed down the gravel road to the river. There were several turns to the left and I was getting confused until I came to the first gate. There was dust ahead of me still hanging in the air as I closed the gate behind me. I thought that if someone else was out here, they might be hunting sage hen too and knew where to go. I would stay on this section of road and follow them.

The only thing I could see ahead of me was dust . The road was tight and moved in and out of small mounds of basalt and rock ledges like the tracks of a roller coaster. Suddenly, the road rose out from the basin and the land opened up before me. I spotted a blue and white late model pickup about a quarter mile out. I pulled to a stop on a small rise and saw two men get out with shotguns and a black Lab. I watched as they moved over a small hill out of sight. I was concentrating on the hill, hoping to see which direction they were headed, when I heard two shots, then three more and saw four large birds fly up the draw and over the next rise. It was 2:00 p.m.

I had an hour to hunt and planned to make the best of it. Quickly gathering up my gun and a handfull of shells, I let Anneca and Beth out the back of the van. We traveled in the direction I had seen the birds flush with hopes of working singles. As we worked along the edge of the river's canyon, I could see the two men and their Lab hunting along the same line. Anneca and Beth spotted the three and kept wanting to head their way. Weaving in and out of the canyon's edge, we finally met the threesome and stopped to talk.

I told them this was my first hunt for sage hen and had come all the way from Boise to hunt for the day. One of the men told me they had another group of hunters over the next rise. They planned to hunt up the draw in the same direction in hopes of pushing any grouse they missed to them. We wished each other luck and went our separate ways.

Anneca and Beth were ranging far out. I tried calling them in but both were too keyed up from the long drive in the van. They were off north to my left near an outcropping of basalt about 60 yards ahead when they bumped two large grouse. The girls acted like they

Beth Cools off.

hadn't seen either grouse and kept on going. I called to them and when I didn't get a response, I started trotting after them. I practically stepped on the next four birds as they exploded from under my feet, sending my first shot straight up into the air. The next shot folded a grouse in a cloud of feathers, hard hit.

Anneca and Beth came running in my direction at the sound of the shot and ran into a group of grouse I estimated to be around forty. The grouse rose as one unit and sailed across the Big Lost to safety on the other side. The girls stopped and watched as the last bird disappeared into the sage, then came to my side. After a short scolding, I showed them both the dead grouse. Their tails were traveling in circles as they stuffed their noses into the slate gray feathers of the grouse and drank in its sweet bouquet. We sat and took a water break before trying to find a way to cross the canyon's vertical walls to the other side.

I was worried Anneca and Beth might overheat from the sun and made sure they were well-rested before moving on. It was in the low eighties with not a cloud in the sky as we worked our way along the edge of the canyon. As I neared the edge, I spotted an antelope dashing out from the far side of the Big Lost's bank and disappear over the rise. This was the place to cross.

It wasn't an easy descent. The wall of the canyon stair stepped down into the banks of the Big Lost. I had to step down to the next ledge, pick up one of the girls, set her down and do the same for the other. At the base of the canyon wall, the Big Lost formed a large, three feet deep pool. I was glad to give Anneca and Beth a chance to cool off in the icy waters. The rest was welcomed. Anneca and Beth splashed and chased each other in the pool. I let them tell me when they were ready to move on and soon they were heading for the opposite bank. They stopped and looked back at me as if to say, "Well, what are you sitting around for? Let's go get something!"

We reached the opposite side and it was clear this was where the antelope had been crossing. There were tracks all along the edge of the water in the soft sand and a heavily worn trail came down from the top. Getting out of the canyon from this side was a lot easier. In no time we were on the flat ground above, working west along the canyon rim. Beth and Anneca were finally hunting like a team, leaving no likely cover uninvestigated.

We'd moved about one hundred yards when Anneca started

getting birdy. She moved another twenty yards and slammed to a stoped as Beth moved in to back. I walked in for the flush, only to have Anneca move ahead to relocate. She moved ahead twice more before skidding to a stop just below a small rise. I worked my way in front of her, thinking that if the birds were running, I could pin them between Anneca and myself. I was twenty yards ahead of her when a group of about thirty grouse flushed some twenty-five yards out. They got up with surprisingly little noise, scattering in every direction. With all the birds in that group, I had trouble concentrating on just one grouse.

Another group of stragglers flushed across in front of me as I dropped the lead grouse with the first shot. I could tell by the way it fell that its wing was broken. With the dry conditions I was con-

Anneca with her bird.

cerned I would lose it. My worries were short lived, however. In the distance I could see Anneca coming back with a grouse so large, it covered up most of her face. She delivered the grouse with style. With a pat on her side and a "good girl", I cast the girls in the direction form where the last group of grouse had flown.

We traveled across the sage and rocky terrain for a half mile

The Sage Grouse ~
Standing on the rocky platue.

before we stopped and took a break. It was getting late. I cast the girls in the direction of the van. We worked our way to a spot where six grouse had flushed across to the other side. Ten yards from the canyon's edge, Beth moved in and slammed to a stop. She had pointed so quickly she was nearly bent in half. Anneca was still working the sage behind Beth and I motioned her in the direction of Beth. As I moved in front of Beth, Anneca came over a small mound and made a beautiful back when she spotted Beth on point. I took another step and a large male sage grouse flushed from the base of a sage, not five yards ahead of Beth. I was ready and he folded before he made it to the other side of the canyon, landing on our side of the Big Lost.

Anneca and Beth scrambled down the basalt wall of the canyon from ledge to ledge as it stair stepped to the water's edge. The grouse was wing-tipped and made it out into the middle of the waterbefore the girls reached it. By the time I made it to the

*Beth ~
rock solid.*

bottom of the canyon, Anneca was already on the shore with the grouse. She delivered it to me, then immediately returned to the water to cool off.

Not willing to backtrack to where we had originally crossed, I decided to take a more direct line to the van and cross the Big Lost from where we were. The walls were steep, but from where I stood, it seemed like a possible climb. When we reached the other side, clearly I had made a mistake. This would be anything but easy. I had to take Anneca and Beth one at a time and literally lift them up the twenty foot canyon wall. I left the gear at the water's edge and took Beth first. Lifting her over my head, I had her stand on a small ledge, told her to stay, then climbed up on the ledge myself. There wasn't enough room to position myself to lift her to the next ledge, so as I moved to the next plateau, I had to grab her by the collar and lift her up to me. Once there, I was able to push her from behind to keep her from slipping on the rocky slope until we reached the top.

It had taken a good ten minutes to reach the top with Beth. After making it, I took a break at the edge of the canyon while Anneca whined on the sandy bank below. Anneca was not as cooperative on the climb up and jumped down twice from the first ledge before I could get her to stay. As we neared the top, Beth was peering over the edge, prancing and whining, encouraging us. After a bit more of a struggle than with the first trip, we finally reached the top. I sat with my feet dangling over the edge, Beth on one side of me and Anneca on the other.

Rested, I left the girls behind and went back for my gun and camera. Anneca and Beth watched me descend and whined back as I disappeared from view.

The climb back to the top was faster alone. When I reached the summit, Anneca and Beth were nowhere in sight. The edge of the canyon was about four feet lower than the surrounding terrain. As I stood up, I spotted two large sage grouse standing on a flat pad of rock thirty feet to the west. The grouse were both looking off to the east. Following their line of sight, I found Beth on point some twenty yards from the grouse, thirty yards further was Anneca on back to Beth's point.

We already had three sage grouse with the last bird so, I took several photos before moving in for the flush. As I walked in, Beth acknowledged me with a glance and returned to the business at hand while Anneca was immobile, honoring Beth's point with style. I came within twenty yards of the birds before they rocketed straight up some fifty yards, then sailed off into the distance. I watched for quite a while, thinking the grouse would tire and land but they kept going until they were out of sight. I wished them well and hoped we might meet again next year. Hot and tired, we walked back to the van.

The rocky ground had taken its toll on Anneca and Beth's pads. While I unloaded the gun and took off my vest, they sat in the shade of the van, licking their feet. I took photos of the girls and their grouse, broke for lunch and took a short rest before making the long drive home.

I've never made it back to the Big Lost, but the chance to hunt those big grouse still calls to me when the leaves begin to change, the days get shorter and the nights get colder.

Anneca and Beth ~
day's end.

Mary's Creek

The Author, Anneca, Beth and Keith Bloom ~
hunting partners.

Mary's Creek

Tucked away between two bluffs of sage and rock, miles from the encroachment of man, lies Mary's Creek. One half mile west of where the road crosses the creek is a remnant of a small ranch house, the outline of the foundation and half the hearth, its only trace. The nearest town, Grasmere, is a small trading post that houses a post office, a small restaurant, and a gas station. It is a popular stop for tour buses on their way to Nevada with gambling parties and last gas for a hundred miles.

It was dark when Keith Bloom and I reached the city limit sign of Grasmere. We drove another thirty minutes before realizing the small building we had seen earlier was Grasmere. Backtracking our way to the Grasmere 'city limits' we found the turn-off to Mary's Creek.

The road was dusty and rough, the land was flat, and Keith kept joking that the creek didn't exist. By the second round of jokes the flat terrain we'd been traveling on opened up before us. It was the creek. The forecast for that weekend called for clouds and heavy rain, but the weather now was mild. With the moon as our flashlight, we set up camp while F11 fighter jets were cruising on night maneuvers, setting an erie tone to the evening. In the distance, the calls of coyotes as they checked each other's location kept the dogs a little on edge. As we set up camp by the light of the moon, Anneca and Beth stayed by my side while Keith's dog, Ben, barked in defiance at the coyotes. The drive out to Mary's Creek was long and leaving late from home made it seem even longer.

The next morning we were awakened by the calls of Valley Quail just outside the tent. Keith slept in while I got up and made breakfast. As the aroma of eggs and bacon filled the campsite, I watched the small covey of quail that I'm sure had awakened us, stroll within twenty feet of camp. The smell of food had coaxed Keith out of his sleeping bag. With half his body hanging out the tent flap, he caught a glimpse of the last few stragglers of the covey disappear into the tall grass along the creek's edge.

"Should we shoot 'em?,"Keith shouted. Because Keith was excited it took me a while to convince him there were plenty more quail in the area. After finishing breakfast, we decided we could hunt the creek more effectively if we split up. With the help of a coin toss, Keith chose the upstream end of the creek and I chose the downstream. I gave Keith time to head up stream so the birds in the area wouldn't get too spooky. Fifteen minutes after Keith had disappeared, three shots echoed down the canyon from his direction. The hunt was on!

Ten minutes from camp Anneca and Beth found a covey of quail I estimated at well over a hundred. The birds were in groups both on the ground and up in the higher branches of willows that lined the creek's edge. Anneca and Beth spotted the birds and slowly moved in towards them only to lock on point a few seconds later. I moved in for the flush. Two Valley Quail took off from the covey's edge. I took a quick shot but parted nothing but air. The rest of the covey scattered like a swarm of bees from a bee hive. Half flushed upstream toward Keith and his dog, Ben, the other half flew across the creek and into the heavier cover downstream. The rest of the morning the girls and I worked up one single and double after another. While working an area some 50 yards above the creek, Anneca locked solid. As I walked in, six birds flushed and I managed to drop one. The rest headed for the creek and the safety of the willows. The ground was very dry, despite the early morning hour, and it was some time before Anneca found the bird. She made a beautiful delivery to hand of a mature cock Valley Quail. With a pat on the side and a "good girl", we were off to find the rest of the covey.

As the girls reached the creek, my eyes focused on the tall grass beyond. Anneca and Beth were working hard and had stopped along the creek's edge to cool off. When I reached their sides, they were panting heavily and lying with their bellies in the cool mud of the creek bank. It was great to be out in an area where I'd never been, hunting new terrain with a surprise around every bend and sitting beside Anneca and Beth. I took a drink of cool water from my canteen, and enjoyed the moment.

After a short rest we headed for the tall grass. As we reached it, a bluish-gray blur rockted from its center and offered a left to right shot. The bird folded at the bark of my twelve gauge and landed in the middle of the creek. Anneca and Beth saw the bird fall and were in the water in a flash. Beth reached the bird first, but it had landed in a seven feet deep portion of the creek. Realizing just how deep the water was, she panicked and started splashing. With all the commotion, the bird disappeared. When Anneca and Beth reached the bank, the bird was nowhere to be found.

The girls shook themselves off and ran to my side. Looking back to the water and not seeing the quail I was disappointed and scolded the two. After a few more moments of scolding I sent the two back down the creek's edge. Anneca ran to the spot where they had left the water, then ran back to me, then ran back to the spot and sat down looking back with that silly grin of hers. Reaching her side, I saw a small puddle of water and a small blue-gray form lying at her feet. After a few apologies and several "good girls, " I cast them toward the open sage and rim rock above the canyon. Making the top of the canyon wall, Anneca and Beth started to range out to about 70 yards. Every so often they'd point, move ahead slowly, then move on again.

After fifteen minutes of the stop and go work, Beth and Anneca locked on point. Thinking this was it-we were finally into sage grouse-I moved causally in a large arc ahead of Anneca and Beth. When I stepped in to flush, nothing materialized. This happened three more times with the same results. Thinking either the birds were running or the dogs were pointing rabbits, I cast the girls back in the direction of the creek.

Reaching the canyon's edge Anneca and Beth went on point. As I walked ahead of them, a group of five quail flushed from under my feet and sailed across the creek to the other side of the canyon. I didn't shoot for fear that if one of the birds dropped, both of the girls might leap over the cliff to retrieve it. Instead, I marked the area where the group landed and traversed down the canyon walls to the far side of the creek. We hunted the area hard, but were unable to find a single quail.

Anneca and Beth were getting tired and I was hungry, so we made our way back to camp for some lunch. When we reached camp there were three Valley Quail hanging from one of the tent poles; the result of the three shots I heard that morning. I had just finished watering the dogs and sat down for lunch when Keith and Ben strolled into camp. "How'd ya do? " I asked.

"Can't hit the broad side of a barn," Keith said. "But I did manage to flush a group of chukar."

He told me of an old abandoned farm he and Ben had run across that had nothing left but the foundation and a few remnant fence posts. It was about a half mile upstream. I told him about the quail we encountered. We decided after a long rest that we would switch locations for a change of pace.

It was 5:00 p.m. when Keith and I woke up. A quick grab of granola and a refill of the canteens and we were off once more. Anneca, Beth and I took our time and left no stand of cover unchecked. It took thirty minutes to reach the farm. As we crossed the fence row, Beth went solid. Anneca made a beautiful back. "This is it", I said to myself and moved in for the flush. As I walked in, Beth broke point and scattered chukar in groups of two and four.

A bird flushed and flew right at me, causing me to duck as it flew over my head. I swung around to my right and dropped it with the first shot. Then quickly turning towards the covey rise, I dropped another with a right-to-left shot. The bird folded and lodged in the forked branch of a willow at the base of the creek. Chukar were flushing in all directions as I frantically tried to reload. Fumbling with the pockets of my game vest, I grabbed two shells, stuffed them into the open gun, and closed the breach just as the last bird flushed. The bird rose from my right. Leveling my gun I put the bead on the chukar, pulled through, and squeezed the trigger. The bird folded in a cloud of feathers.

Anneca and Beth were still searching for the other two birds as the last hit the ground. Feathers were hanging in the air as Anneca delivered the first bird to hand. I waved Beth to the last bird, but before she could pick it up, Anneca snatched it from under her nose and layed it at my feet. The second bird had landed in the willow branches and was impossible for the girls to find in the dry conditions. I finally walked over to the willows and plucked the bird from the forked branch myself.

Keith was already in camp when the girls and I wandered in. After a short recounting of the day's events, we started dinner. The main course: chukar stuffed with sauerkraut, raisins and walnuts. While I prepared the birds, Keith started the dessert: homemade blueberry muffins. He made a fire, placed the muffin batter in aluminum foil and set it in the middle of the fire on a flat rock. The chukar was cooked in a Dutch oven on the camp stove, smothered with the last of the sauerkraut to keep the meat moist and tender.

The day had taken its toll on all of us. Anneca, Beth, and Ben's pads were red and sore from the volcanic rock and cactus in the area and Keith and I were stiff from the uneven footing. As daylight faded and the fire grew brighter, we sat in its warm glow and ate, reflecting on the day's hunt. Clouds rolled in, the temperature dropped and the wind picked up, making it almost impossible to keep loose camp items from blowing away. The weather was turning for the worst. We moved dinner inside the tent and settled down for a long rest.

Keith had been having tooth problems, so we decided to cut tomorrow's hunt short. The next day was overcast, cool and mostly uneventful. Keith and Ben managed to jump one quail. Keith made a great shot, dropping the bird into the cold waters of the creek. Ben made the first retrieve of his young life. With the bird in hand, we agreed to cut our losses and head back to town. We broke camp and left the creek before 10:00 a.m., all of us with sore muscles and a feeling of satisfaction and accomplishment.

Part Two: Close to Home

Coyote Creek

The Author, Anneca and Beth ~
in the clouds.

Coyote Creek

Coyote Creek holds special meaning for me. Close to home, no more than an hour away, it was the first area I hunted with Anneca and Beth for grouse and it produced for many years. In the late seventies and early eighties, this area was mostly untouched by the local population and I took great measures to keep it a secret. I considered it my private covert and reserved it only for my father, brother and myself. Anneca made her first point on grouse in this area; an encounter that set her blood on fire and kept it burning bright for twelve years.

The other day while cleaning out the basement, I came across a stack of old Super 8 movies. The plastic canisters protecting the film were covered with dust, all but forgotten in a pile of memorabilia. During my cleaning I had also uncovered the projector. I randomly grabbed a roll of film, dusted off the cover's description to read "*Anneca and Beth 1980.*" I loaded the film in the projector, plugged it in, pointed it at the bare wall and flicked the switch. The old projector hummed and clicked as the film fed into the catch reel, the light from inside cutting a path through the darkness while dust particles danced in it.

As I watched, a hazy memory of the day struggled to reveal itself. The film was of one of the first hunts for Huns at Daniel's Creek. Anneca and Beth moved at a surrealistic pace, as everything does on old film, while I panned the horizon and tryed to keep up with them. There was a glitch in the film and suddenly I was transported to Coyote Creek. Anneca was weaving her way through aspens and chokecherries with my dad following behind her. She stopped to look back at me, then the film came to an end.

Sitting there in the dark while the film slapped against the projector, I tried to remember that day but couldn't. It was like it had never happened; I had watched someone else's father hunt with one of my dogs. After sitting there in the dark for a while, I decided to look through my shooting diary in hopes of finding an entry that might help jar my memory. There was no entry that matched, although I did find the entry of Anneca and Beth's first hunt at Coyote Creek:

October 10,1980.

The girls and I left Boise this morning at 10:30 and made the hour-long drive to Coyote Creek on a hunt for Blue grouse. Reaching the lower lodge of Bogus Basin, a local ski resort, I stopped to look over the number one chair lift. The sky was clear and the air crisp--what a time to be out with the dogs and a familiar gun!

We took the washboard road that winds around the back side of the mountain. Just as the resort was disappearing in the rear view mirror, a female Blue crossed the road in front of us. As I drove past, the bird scrambled up the slope of the road into a patch of chokecherries. I stopped to let the girls out in hopes of getting a chance at their first point on grouse. But as the girls left the back of the van, the grouse flushed across the road and disappeared into the canyon below. When they reached the area where the Blue had been, they both went on solid point. A good start, I thought to myself, as I put the girls back into the van and continued our drive to Coyote Creek.

We'd gone less than a quarter mile when we jumped a pair of big 'Blues' from the side of the road. The first grouse sailed into the trees below., The second landed in the low branches of a fir at the side of the road. I stopped the van, gathered up two shells and the over/ under then slipped out the door. As I rounded the rear of the van, the grouse spotted me and stretched out on the branch in an attempt to hide. While I walked towards the bird, the girls were making all sorts of noise trying to find a way out of the van so they could join me. This was more than the grouse could handle. As I drew closer, he flew off in classic Blue grouse fashion -- thundering wing beats that offered little chance of a shot.

My pattern caught the bird just before it reached the safety of the dense fir below. He tumbled down the steep slope and rested at the base of a large deadfall. I returned to the van and let Anneca and Beth out to locate and retrieve the downed bird. After a short search, Anneca found the grouse and made a sweet delivery. Taking the bird from her mouth, I held it over her head and told her what a good gird she was. Then, with a pat on the head and another "good girl," we walked back to the van and were on the road again.

It was another twenty minutes of teeth-rattling washboard road before we reached a special spot where my dad and I had hunted the year before. There were Blues in this area last year in groups of ten and more. I hoped we would be as lucky today. I parked just shy of the cattle guard, watered up the girls and headed for the fire trail on the north side of the slope. We worked our way into an area filled with choke cherries. The hillside was protected from the sun and the air was cool. Anneca and Beth covered every inch of ground. Although I had flushed a group of sixteen in this very spot the year before, today we produced nothing.

The girls left no stand of cover unchecked. With the air thin and our excitement high, we stopped for a water break. The view was spectacular. From our seat among the chokecherries we could see all the way to the Sawtooth Mountain Range. Anneca and Beth lied on their sides, chests heaving from the bite of the mountain air, yet I could see the enjoyment in their faces...that silly grin. Time was running out, so after a short break we were on the move again.

As we made the rise, we came to the base of a small stand of fir. Beth locked on point next to a large dead fall just shy of the firs. It wasn't a solid point; the tip of her tail wagged slightly as she moved ahead to relocate. Several more flash points and Beth lost interest so we moved on. The cover was getting thicker, which would make shooting difficult if we got into grouse. I called the girls in and cast them up the ridge above us.

As we reached the summit, Anneca and Beth took off back towards the van. They were soon out of sight, but their bells chimed their location as they moved through the stands of aspen and fir. The duo of brass soon turned to a solo. Beth was below below me working a small creek bed. I called her back from the creek bed and gave her a short rest when she reached my side. We then headed in the direction I had last heard Anneca's bell.

We crossed through a small stand of aspen and broke into the open. There at the base of a large fir, whose branches reached the ground, was Anneca on the most beautiful and grand point I had ever seen. With her head high and her tail stretched stiff as a board, she searched the air for the sweet sent of grouse. When Beth spotted Anneca she slowed, took a few steps forward and made a picture-perfect back. I moved in for the flush. As I drew closer, a brace of Blue grouse rocketed from beneath the base of the fir; not five yards in front of Anneca and headed downhill.

Through some miracle I managed to pull off two shots and the brace folded and fell out of sight down the steeply sloping terrain. Anneca and Beth were on the grouse before I could form the words 'dead bird'. By the time I reached the base of the fir, Anneca was already on her way up the with the first bird. Beth was still searching the cover for the second when Anneca delivered the first, blue dun breast with a slate-gray tail. Both birds were mature Blue grouse, male and female. Beth finally managed to locate the second bird. With that, we sat down for a water break and a breather.

After a short rest and a few snapshots to record the event, we made our way back to the van for some lunch. Our bellies full and our muscles rested, we crossed the road and made our way south. About halfway up the ridge Beth and Anneca bumped into a group of about six Blue grouse. The birds got up in front of a patch of chokecherries between the girls and me. I took a desperation shot through the brush, but never parted a feather.

We followed the last bird's line of flight. After a steep climb, we came to an open park with high grass scattered with an occasional patch of chokecherry. Anneca and Beth were covering ground well at about thirty yards out. As I reached the center of the park, I motioned the girls to start back down towards the road. The moment we started down, I kicked up a big male Blue grouse that practically flushed from under my feet.

The flush caught me off guard and by the time I was able to shoulder my gun, the grouse was well out ahead. I managed two shots that hit the bird both times, but the big Blue kept flying. Feathers were still hanging in the air as we watched the grouse sail out of sight into the pines below--the trouble of using #8s on such a large bird.

It was a short distance to the van, but the walk out was difficult. Following a spring creek that was in direct line with the bird's flight, we followed up with hopes of relocating the bird, but no luck. Tired and hungry, we headed back to the van and took another lunch break. With the sun setting on the horizon, we headed back home.

Anneca ~
her first grouse.

The Creeks

Cabin Creek

Beth and Anneca ~
end of a day's hunt at The Cabin.

Cabin
Creek

Cabin Creek empties into the Daniel's miles below Coyote Creek. The range of bird species over laps into this area which supports Chukar partridge, Ruffed grouse and Mountain quail. Anneca and Beth had glorious hunts in these hills just below the tree line - their first point on Ruffed grouse, first encounter with Mule deer and first points on Mountain quail. The quail have disappeared, but the grouse and chukars are still there.

The other day I was going through some old slides and found a picture of Anneca and Beth with two brace of Ruffed grouse. It stirred up memories that needed to be relived. Dusting off one of my old gun dog diaries, I found a passage to match the picture:

November 15, 1983: Drove to the headwaters of Cabin Creek this afternoon. There wasn't enough time, but made the trip anyway. We were out for chukar and huns and a chance atMountain quail.

Haven't seen any quail since last year. Wonder where they've gone?

The drive in was a short twenty minutes. I was in one of my reflective moods. As I drove, I kept asking myself if I was giving all that I could to Anneca and Beth to make their lives complete. Is there ever enough time? There was a foot of snow on the ground as I pulled to the side of the switch-back to park. As I stepped from the van to let the girls out, four cars filled with skiers waved and bid us good luck.

Clouds had rolled in, softening everything in grays and blues. The walk back was quiet. We were the only ones out in this great basin. Not another boot track to be found -- the canyon was ours! We traveled the steep slope leading to the cabins and the headwaters below. As we traversed the hillside, we left the hustle and bustle of the working world behind. We were alone. The cover was good, but beneath the snow were hidden demon stumps and branches. I fell more than once on the way in. We jumped three does half-way back. They crashed down the slope to the creek, making the other side in a matter of seconds, while Anneca and Beth watched with indifference. We worked to the end of the draw. As the footing got worse and the snow grew deeper, we struggled up the opposite side to the willows above.

We cut across a deer trail half way up and followed it out to thinner cover. The trail took us to a small park that intersected a jeep trail. The grade was steep but far easier walking. We used the trail to access the upper portions of the drainage 800 yards above us. At the top was a switch back cutting across the saddle that con- nected the two ridges between Stack Rock and the cabins. The east side had good cover, concentrated in a tight space 40 yards across. Mid way to the saddle Anneca started getting birdy. She moved twenty yards ahead and locked up solid at the edge of a drop off. Beth moved in from behind and slid to a stop, honoring Anneca's point.

I walked in for the flush. Anneca and Beth's tails were wagging then both broke point, moved ahead ten yards and looked back at me. Moving to meet them, I caught a movement on the hill across the draw. I saw nothing for a moment, then it moved again - a small herd of mule deer and just below, the three does we had jumped earlier. We stood and watched as the three joined the herd then disappear over the next rise.

The climb had taken its toll and as the last deer faded from view, we sat down for another break before moving up the trail. I munched

Anneca ~ her quail.

on a pheasant sandwich while Beth and Anneca had their two Oreo cookies to keep their blood sugars up. We finished off with a cool drink from the canteen and a couple of bites of fresh snow. I had planned to climb to the saddle, but as we came closer,

I could see the cover was less than what I had expected. A small trickle of a creek was gurgling through the small draw clung tightly by willows and groups of elderberries. On the far side was a lone pine tree; the start of the tree line above.

Beth made her way to the opposite side, while Anneca worked the draw up the creek toward the tree line. As Anneca reached a dense group of willows, I could see her flash point. She moved ahead, jerked to her right and froze. There was a flutter of wings as the snow on the branches above her fell to the ground around her. Calling Beth in with a whistle, I motioned her into the willows. She entered just below Anneca, immediately caught scent and froze up next to Anneca. A double point!

I hadn't seen anything exit the willows when the bird flushed. I moved in closer, searching the dense upper branches for a sign of game. Then I spotted it. Twenty feet ahead of the girls and ten feet above, a Ruffed grouse peered down at them through the entanglement of willow. I took another step and it saw me, its crest erect, ready for flight. Another second passed and the silence was broken by the explosion of wings as the grouse headed for the safety of the pines above. The grouse dropped in a cloud of feathers at about twenty yards, hard hit, falling at the base of the lone pine. Feathers were still hanging in the air as Anneca found the bird, brought it back, and laid it at my feet. We sat at the base of the huge pine and admired the bird, brown and tan with jet black ruffs. It was a mature male. We took a water break and had a quick snack before moving on to the northeast side of the canyon.

As we climbed higher towards the tree line above, clouds started rolling from the west, the temperature dropped and it began to snow. The storm was light at first, but it progressively became worse. Visibility was limited to about two hundred yards as we worked from one draw to the next. I was letting the girls work cover with a limited amount of control on my part, letting them go where they would. At the third draw over we came to a line of aspens and buckbrush at the edge of the sage. Anneca and Beth had just come up from the last deep draw and I called them to my location, fifty yards above. There was another small creek at the bottom of the draw. We sat at its edge for a short rest and drink before moving on. The snow had stopped, but the clouds dropped down to hug the ground around us, wrapping everything in a dense fog. I then made the decision to hunt a line of aspens to the bottom of the draw and work our way back to the van. We hadn't traveled more than fifty yards when Anneca disappeared into the aspens. Beth was following her. As she approached the spot where Anneca had entered, Beth slammed to a stop. I could still hear Anneca's bell, but she was moving very slowly. Within thirty seconds all was quiet; bird number two was pinned down some where ahead.

I was twenty yards from Beth when the grouse flushed in front of Anneca. Surprisingly, instead of heading for thick cover, it flew for the open sage. I pulled my gun on the grouse, swung through the bird and squeezed the trigger. It was out a good thirty yards when I shot. I must have aimed high because it kept on going. My second shot caused the grouse to falter, quickly lose altitude and then disappear below the slope. It fell in deep snow some eighty yards from where it had flushed. Anneca and Beth were down in the aspens when the birds had flushed and hadn't seen it fall. Worried the bird would be lost to the distance and the deep snow, as Anneca reached my side I quickly cast her downhill on a blind retrieve.

She fell short on the first cast. I moved her on with a wave of my hand and the command 'back.' Anneca looked at me for a moment as if to consider, then spun around and faded from sight over the rise. Her bell had filled up with snow, so I had no idea where she was as she searched the cover below, lost from view. My worries were short lived. Within a few minutes Anneca returned over the rise with her bird. I proudly thought to myself, "She never fails me." We paused a moment to collect ourselves. As daylight faded, we headed down to the main creek.

I had every intintion of heading back to the van, but Beth and Anneca had other ideas. Crossing the creek, they made a direct line for a group of thick blue green fir, a stark contrast agianst the white snow. I wanted to move them on to the van, but as they reached the firs, they both were acting very birdy so, so I followed them. As Anneca disappeared into the stand of pine, I heard a grouse flush upthe hill. I quickly headed in the direction of the bird's flight and began to search for Anneca and Beth.

After the last grouse, I had taken the time to clean the snow from the girls' bells. Clear bells helped greatly as I followed Anneca and Beth through the thick brush. The grade was steep and I fell twice on the frozen ground. After climbing forty yards, I was close enough, for a few seconds, to catch a glimpse of the two disappearing over the next plateau. Anneca was working to my right and Beth to my left. As I climbed higher, I spotted Beth working a deer trail, then she disappeared into a dense thicket of willow. Her bell went silent. I quickly made an arch above her and moved in, ready to shoot. Reaching a clearing, I could see her below me standing in the middle of the trail, pointing solidly. When I reached her side, she broke point, moved a few yards ahead, and locked up once more.

The wind was coming up from the creek below. As I moved closer to Beth, I could see her nostrils flaring and eyes bulging out. The bird was close by. I tried moving her on but she wouldn't budge. With every step that I took around her, she would tense her muscles and flinch. I expected the grouse to flush with each step, but nothing came of it. I moved in ahead of her. She broke point again, frantically covering ground for a trace of sent. Anneca came from the cover above me and moved to my side. She too, went on point. But there was something different about the way she held her ground. Something in her eyes.

Beth turned back and looked uphill. I motioned her to me with two quick waves on my hand. Halfway up she spotted Anneca and froze to honor. I tried to send Anneca on but she would have nothing to do with it. Then I noticed her eyes again. She was looking at something. Following her line of sight, some twelve feet above Beth, I spotted two Ruffed grouse feeding on buds in the upper branches of the willows. As one of the birds moved to another branch, Anneca caught the movement and slowly changed her back to a point. The two grouse, who had been oblivious to our presence until now, spotted Beth and froze, their crests erect, positioned for flight.

Raising my gun to port of arms, I took another step towards Anneca. As I did, both grouse took of in a thunder of beating wings, heading for the stand of fir below. I took the first bird with the upper barrel, folding it clean at twenty yards. Anneca broke point as I took the second shot at thirty five yards. The grouse

'Havent seen any quail since last year'

was definitely hit. A few feathers were knocked off its back and it faltered before disappearing into the dense fir below.

The momentum of the first bird's flight took it to the base of the creek. I rushed to the bottom in hopes of finding the second. Anneca and Beth were allready returning with the first grouse when I reached the creek. Anneca had it, the darkest ruffed grouse

I had ever seen.Beth was ahead of Anneca. As they made their way to me, she looked over her shoulder at Anneca with indiference. Anneca delivered the bird to me, then we all sat at the base of a large fir to rest before trying to locate the second grouse.

We ate the last of the treats I had packed for the day's hunt as I searched the trees for a glimpse of the grouse. I looked back to the spot where I had shot and tried to retrace the bird's line of flight. We searched for the grouse for twenty minutes before returning to the fir; taking one last rest before heading to the van some six hundred yards above.

I had just stod up to stretch my legs when the most amazing thing happened. From up in the top branches of the tree came a fluttering of wings. The ruffed grouse I had shot a half hour earlier fell at me feet, dead as a stone! After examining the bird, I found that two number 8s had penetrated its back - a lung shot. Apparently it had flown into the tree to hide and had taken all that time to expire.

We gathered up what remaining strength we had and made the long climb to the back to the van. Ther were more grouse in the area and we spotted several down below the tree line on the way out. We didn't hunt The Cabin for the rest of the year, leaving the grouse undisturbed, ready to hunt next season.

The Creeks

Stack Rock

Anneca and Beth ~
at the base of Stack Rock.

Stack Rock

Stack Rock is a few short minutes from my house. Set three miles off the main road to a local ski resort, it goes all but unnoticed. I discovered this area on a day hike in the early seventies. First hunted in the fall of 1974, I didn't hunt 'the rock' again for five years. Strong populations of Valley quail, Hungarian partridge, and Chukar partridge lie along the trail that leads to the base of Stack Rock and throughout it. At its base there is a rocky outline of the remains of an old ranch house flanked by three plum trees and two black walnut trees.

The east face of 'the rock,' along with the ranch foundation, has several springs that feed a small creek. It runs through the flats at the base of Stack Rock and creates a small oasis in otherwise dry and arid land.

Reading through my gun diary I came across Anneca and Beth's first hunt there, November 19, 1979:

I took the girls out hunting quail and chukar this afternoon at Stack Rock. It had snowed last night at the four thousand foot elevation which, I decided, would get the birds out and about today. Anneca and Beth had never seen snow. They played and chased each other as I gathered my gear for the three mile trek to the base of 'the rock.' The trail to the base was mostly downhill and the girls left no likely cover untouched.

When we reached the ranch house foundation we broke for lunch, a sandwich for me, hamburger balls for the girls. It was reassuring to be on familiar ground. Rested, we started upstream toward the east side of the ranch. We'd gone no more than a few hundred yards when clouds dropped into the valley and it began to snow and hail. We sat under a large plum tree until the storm let up before moving on.

Working our way farther upstream, we came to a bend in the creek next to a large cottonwood tree and several scattered clumps of willow. Beth was twenty feet ahead of me when she stopped in mid-stride and locked solid on point as Anneca backed. I took two steps forward. A covey of about ten Valley quail flushed from my left. I took two shots, dropping a mature cock with the first and parting air with the second. The covey split, half headed downstream towards the ranch house, the rest made their escape up the steep grade and disappeared into the fog. The girls followed suit. I called the girls in, took a short rest to calm them down and then moved up stream, figuring we would work the singles on our way back.

As we made our way up the draw, Anneca and Beth kept moving uphill. Because of the steep grade, I called them back to work the willows along the creek's edge. After several failed attempts to keep them in the willows, I gave in and followed them up the steep grade towards the cliffs. This uphill climb was rough. The girls and I were getting hot despite the two inches of snow on the ground. I called the girls in and we took a short rest on the snowy hillside.

Beth and Anneca were still pups and needed no excuse to goof around. Anneca was the first to start. She rolled on her back and squirmed back and forth on the steep grade until her weight compacted the snow beneath her until down the hill she went! It didn't take Beth too long to catch on and soon they were both sliding downhill on their backs. I was getting hot too and took a break to watch the girls cool off. I sat and watched the girls play for about fifteen minutes before we moved higher.

We were a hundred and fifty feet below the base of Stack Rock when Beth saw chukar or caught sent of them. She took a few steps, then went on point. Anneca backed. I was to their right and directly below a large boulder. Nothing was in sight ahead of me as I worked my way up and around the boulder ahead of the girls. After a few steps, Anneca and Beth were out of sight. Two more steps and chukar began flying out from behind the boulder one at a time and landed twenty yards in front of me.

I dropped the next double, then all hell broke loose. The birds started flushing -- one, two and three at a time. Fumbling to reload, I dropped the first shell in the snow. As birds still flew from behind the boulder, I shoved two shells into the over/under, closed the breach and swung on the next two birds in sight -- a second clean double. Another chukar got up from the left and flew to the safety of the rocks above. The bird folded as it reached the top of the cliffs, then dropped on the flats above.

Chukar were flying in every direction ahead of the girls but they didn't break point. The last bird to get up flew to my right, around the cliff and into a small draw. I called the girls in and sent Anneca to locate the downed birds beneath the cliffs. She delivered the last chukar, then we sat down for a short break before following up the singles. Winded from the multiple retrieves she had made, Anneca sat at my side with a silly grin reflecting a job well done.

As our pulse returned to normal, we followed the line of flight of the last chukar. Working our way to the base of the cliffs, we rounded the corner of the rock's edge and moved into the small draw. As we entered the draw, the bird spotted us and flushed downhill from left to right and headed for the creek below. It folded in a cloud of feathers. Anneca made the retrieve and we sat on the hillside and listened for the calls of the scattered chukar as they tried to regroup the covey.

Five minutes passed before we heard the first bird.

The calls were coming from above us. I listened again and could hear several more calls, all from the top of the plateau. Marking the direction of the calls, we worked our way along the base of the cliff in search of the easiest route to the top. One hundred yards ahead there was a small break in the rock. On our way to the top, just five yards from the edge, were bird tracks in the new fallen snow. The chukar were close. I reached the top and stood motionless, searching for movements among the rocks. Nothing. Two more steps and up jumped a wounded chukar, fluttering and chapping as it made its escape to the edge of the cliff.

I called out 'dead bird' to Anneca and Beth and the chase was on. They were hesitant to retrieve because the chukar was fluttering and chirping. They would get close enough to grab the bird, then it would jump up and the girls would back off. The chase ran to the edge of the cliff, then the chukar tumbled off the edge and was lost in the rocks. I called the girls back in, told them what good girls they were for making a valiant chase, calmed them down, then cast them on.

We walked a short distance. As we climbed over a rise, we flushed a small covey of chukar. I managed to get off a quick shot and dropped the bird over the next rise. Anneca and Beth followed the rest of the covey. After a short chase, I was able to call them back in. I gave the command 'dead bird' and cast them in the direction of the fallen bird, but after a lengthy search the chukar did not materialize. Reluctantly I sent the girls on.

We worked our way into an area of scattered rock. Before I realized it, were on the edge of an almost sheer cliff. The wind came up from the valley below when Beth caught sent of a group of chukar. Before I could stop her, she dove of the cliff's edge, sliding and bouncing off boulders as she went. Once she reached the bottom, she walked a few yards and went on point.

Taking Anneca by the collar, I inched down the rocky ledge. Halfway down, the chukar became nervous and flushed ten yards ahead of Beth, flew across the valley and disappeared around the far end of Stack Rock. We followed their line of flight, but were unable to relocate the covey. It was turning dark, so we began our long walk back to the van.

As we reached the creek, we came to an area of wild grapes just above. Beth locked on point. Anneca backed. I walked in for the flush but, the birds were moving. As I walked past Beth, she moved ahead to relocate and Anneca rushed forward, honoring all the way. I worked my way around them, ready for the flush.

The small covey of Valley quail got up sooner than I had expected. Lead never parted feather despite two tries. One quail flew downstream into the willows that lined the creek inspected us from his perch. I made several attempts to flush the bird by throwing rocks into the willows but had no success. As my supply of rocks diminished, I decided to change tactics.

Playing it cool, I gathered up the girls and led them at heel, pretending I didn't see the quail as I walked towards him. He flushed before I was ready. Anneca and Beth hadn't initially seen the bird, but the flush caught their attention. They followed the quail downstream and dove back into the willows. We walked past the area where he landed when he flushed from behind us. I managed to swing around and dropped him with the first shot. Anneca and Beth took off in the direction of the shot. I called out 'dead bird' as Beth reached the area where the quail had fallen.

Beth started to reach down to retrieve, but Anneca rushed in and grabbed the quail from under her and trotted over to drop it at my feet. On our way back to the van, Beth pointed a covey of Hungarian partridge, but they flushed out of range.

By the time we made it back to the van, the sun had already fallen behind the horizon. Tired and hungry, we headed home.

The Creeks

Quail Creek

Anneca and Beth ~
Double Point.

Quail Creek

Quail Creek is one of those great coverts that at first glance appears not to be worth the time to slow the car down, let alone get out and hunt. But take another look and you'll find that it is the only water and food source for about a mile and holds some of the thickest cover in about the same distance. I've hunted this spot very carefully, making sure not to over hunt. I saved it for special trips, mostly solitary ones. Looking through my gun diary, I found the first entry on the hollow -- December 9, 1979:

My brother Mike and I took Anneca and Beth to hunt Huns and quail this afternoon in the foothills about twenty minutes from the house. We had no sooner reached the area we were to hunt and let the girls out of the van , when Beth went on point. Moving to her right, I crossed the fence at the base of a hill and worked my way ahead of her. When nothing happened, Beth moved ahead of me and pointed once more. I moved ahead of her again and again nothing happened. Beth pointed a third time with no results and I sent her on.

We worked to the top of the hill. When we came to a small basin, a group of chukar flushed a hundred yards below, just a hundred and sixty yards from where Beth had originally pointed. The birds had ran. Mike took Beth down to where the chukar had flushed and jumped two more birds, then shot twice but missed. We hunted the rest of the draws in the area. Failing to locate any more chukar, we headed back in the direction of the van.

On our way back, we jumped a covey of about fifty valley quail feeding on tender grass shoots at the base of the fence along the edge of the road. We reached the van, loaded up the girls and drove about a hundred yards past the quail, let the girls out and then worked our way back towards them. As we got closer, the birds flushed far ahead of us. Two landed in a large patch of wild rose. As Anneca worked her way to the patch, the two quail flushed before she could make point. The first quail flushed straight towards me; the other flushed back over the hill. I dropped the first quail with the first shot. Anneca hadn't seen the bird fall and took off after the second.

After several attempts to call her back, I finally managed to put her in the general area of the fallen bird. I could see the quail lying in the short grass ahead of me and called out 'dead bird.' Even though they were covering ground well, I couldn't direct them to the darned thing. Giving up, I walked over to the bird, set my gun down, and bent over to pick it up. As I reached for the bird, it blinked its eyes, jumped up and flew to the safety of the next ridge!

We hunted the area until dark, but the girls never relocated the birds. Mike managed to take a quick shot at a quail that flushed from the rose hemp and thought he knocked it down. Mike, Anneca Beth and I searched for several minutes, but nothing materialized. We loaded up the girls and headed home.

The great thing about finding a covert like Quail Creek is the accessibility and the anonymity it provides. Too many times an excited hunter who finds an area like this tends to brag on his success. Coverts such as this should be kept secret, cherished and hunted lightly. Limits and numbers are unimportant; it's the quality of the hunt that matters. By keeping the pressure low, by hunting once a week or once every two weeks, a hunter can make a short hunt that allows him to concentrate on the bird work, rather than walking for hours hoping for a chance encounter.

Once a person discovers an area like Quail Creek, a person needs to do his homework. Upland birds, like any other wild animal, have their habits. They tend to use the same area for water, the same area for feed and the same area for bedding down. Get to know the area well, don't over hunt it and as long as there is feed, water and cover, the game will stay put.

A week later I hunted the creek for the second time, but this outing I stopped the van a hundred yards short in hopes of getting the drop on the quail. I watered Anneca and Beth, put their collars on and walked them at heel to the barbed wire fence on the other side of the gravel road. As we crossed the fence, the wind was blowing from Quail Creek. "Perfect", I thought to myself and cast the girls to the edge of cover.

No sooner had I cast Anneca and Beth, when Beth went on point. She locked up solid , then broke, then moved ahead slowly, stopped several times, then worked around the west side onto a cattle trail and then went out of view. I could still hear her bell as she moved through the dense rose hep when I spotted about a dozen Valley quail running along the fence at the edge of the road on the opposite side of the hep. They flushed at the sight of Anneca and me. I motioned to Anneca to head for the fence row and could still hear Beth's bell ringing from across the hep as I crossed the fence and made my way along the road.

Anneca and I reached the end of the rose hep without moving a single bird. We backtracked a bit and I worked Anneca into the middle of the patch with the wind to her advantage. As I watched Anneca work her way though the serpentine tangle of rose vines, it became apparent that only a dog could navigate such an entanglement of thorns. If Anneca was to set on point, there would be no way of flushing the bird myself... it would be up to Anneca.

At my present location it would be next to impossible to take a decent shot if a covey was spotted. The opposite side however, offered an elevated view of the entire area and a clear shot. Quickly I made my way to the other side, only to find Beth on point near a tangle of rose hep, thorns and a fallen log. As I made my way towards her, I could hear the quail start to move and chirp their alarm call.

Reaching Beth's side, the quail flushed from the other side of the log and headed for a large cottonwood tree in the center of the rose hep patch. A plump cock valley quail folded at the bark of my twelve gauge, then another; a few more seconds and they would have been on the other side of the tree along with the rest of the covey.

Although I had impressed myself with the two quick shots, I was a little worried Anneca and Beth would have problems retrieving the quail from the dense cover. My worries were short lived. Without hesitation Anneca and Beth went into the thorny tangle. They caught the sent of the fallen birds in no time. Searching for a break in the thorns, they crawled on their bellies, located the birds and brought them to hand.

A fine performance ended, we walked back to the van together, had a cool drink from the water jug, then made the short drive back home.

Day's end on Quail Creek.

The Creeks

Daniel's Creek

Beth on point ~
Anneca honoring.

Daniel's Creek

I live in an area that offers a variety of game bird species to hunt just a short drive away from my house. Daniel's Creek is a spot where Anneca and Beth had their first experiences on chukar and Huns, performances that will forever live in my memory. It's one of the many special places the three of us discovered during the first few years we began hunting wild birds, and it kept producing until human population increased and development took over.

The dirt and gravel road that we travel is now mostly paved and the majority of the land surrounding the creek has been either posted with no hunting signs or bought up by Californians - most distasteful. But in the early eighties, there were birds at Daniel's Creek and Anneca and Beth had their share of them.

It was September 24, 1980, when we first arrived at this wonderful haunt. Searching through the pages of my gun diary and reading the entry for this day's hunt brought back a flood of memories:

Took the girls to Daniel's Creek in search of chukar and Huns. We hunted from noon to three P.M.. The weather was dry and hot, with a deep turquoise sky and not a breath of breeze. The drive was short... about twenty minutes, and as I passed the dry creek bed that signals the end of the line, I noticed the creek had an unusually large amount of water flowing through its normally bone dry stones.

We turned off to an area known to have small populations of chukar and Huns. I maneuvered the van through the bottom of a steep draw and stopped just short of a willow-lined creek.

Anneca and Beth were excited from the short time in the van. As I gathered gear for the walk in, they ran around the van, chasing each other. It took some time to calm them down and put their collars on before making the long trek up and down the arid hills of sage and cheat grass.

Working our way up the first ridge with no success, we stopped on the far east edge for a rest before starting down to a small trickle of a creek that empties into the larger Daniel's Creek. When our pulse returned to normal, we made our way down to the base and began following the small creek upstream.

Anneca and Beth were fifty yards ahead when I lost sight of them in a large patch of sage on the left side of the creek. Reaching the sage, I found Anneca on the opposite side, working the cover behind me. I motioned her to my side and called Beth in for another rest and a cool drink from the canteen. As we sat, I searched the silence for calls of distant groups of chukar -- calls that never materialized. Our thirst quenched, we moved deeper into the canyon.

We'd gone no more than twenty yards when Beth went on point and Anneca moved in only to lock solid as she spotted Beth whitewashed against the blue-green sage. I was so surprised to see Beth on point, I half doubted her integrity. I walked into the sage and asked inquisitively 'what ya got there girl?' The sound of my voice set a covey of Hungarian partridge into a panic that unraveled my nerves. I managed somehow to pull of two quick shots, missing with the first and folding one Hun with the other. While Anneca retrieved, Beth and I marked the flight of the birds as they dropped into a small basin at the base of a ridge. Anneca made the delivery to hand and with a few 'good girls' we began the trek across the sage to the basin.

The birds were in plain view when we rounded the bend into

the basin and flushed at the sight of Anneca and Beth who were a good seventy yards from them. Their flight was short and steep as they made their way to the top of the ridge. But the telltale sign of the last members of the covey when they arched quickly as they reached the summit told me they had landed. I called the girls back after a short chase, let them cool off with another drink from the canteen and settled them down before we started the steep climb to the covey.

When we neared the summit, some fifteen yards from the top, the girls made scent. With tails wagging and heads held high searching the breeze for the sweet scent of game, Beth locked solid just shy of the top. Not wanting to speak for fear I'd cause another wild flush, I watched anxiously as Anneca made her way toward Beth on the opposite side, out of her line of sight. Anneca reached the summit, caught sent and locked up as well -- a double point!

As I closed the distance between the girls and me, my heart began to race. I kept saying to myself, "concentrate and let's get a double out of this one." I moved in from behind Anneca and made an arc ahead of her, anticipating the explosion of the covey rise. Two more steps and all hell broke loose. Huns scattered around my feet, causing me to shoot too quickly. The first shot, hit nothing but air. The second shot folded a Hun that dropped out of sight and landed in the creek bed below. Watching the rest of the covey scatter into a small patch of willows on the opposite side of the canyon, I stood wondering how in the world I was going to collect the Hun that lie limp somewhere on the stream bed below.

I called Beth to my side and began calling for Anneca, but she was nowhere to be seen. The slope where the bird had fallen was a strong forty five percent, but to my surprise I glimpsed a patch of white working through the sage brush up the hillside towards us. It was Anneca! Super retrieve! We sat at the top of the peak and took a well- deserved rest with water and a few bites from a chocolate bar. I then planned the best route for working the rest of the covey.

At the base of the canyon a small creek crossed a narrow service road. The road wound up the far side of the canyon to the west end of Stack Rock and passed two hundred yards to the east of the willows where the covey had landed. We made our way to where the road crossed the creek, sloshed across the icy water, and walked up the other side to the bend in the road that met the willows, then walked over its edge. Anneca made point in a deep cut in the hillside. As I walked in, two Huns flushed. One headed uphill, the other rocketed down to the safety of the creek. The first dropped clean. Swinging on the second bird, who was nearing the end of the effective range, I held beneath it and squeezed off a second shot. The bird faltered for a moment, then pitched downhill, bouncing and fluttering among the rocks below. Anneca was on the uphill bird while Beth set off for the Hun among the rocks. After Anneca delivered the first bird to hand, I sent her to the creek to help Beth with the second bird. Ten minutes passed before Anneca and Beth were able to locate the Hun, air-washed and limp among the rocks.

The temperature had climbed into the upper eighties and we risked overheating if we were to continue hunting, so we headed for the van. Although we hadn't connected on chukar, the trip was well worth the time.

The Creeks

When

Beth and Anneca ~
the twilight of life.

When

There is always the question of when the time will come when you have to decide to call it quits on hunting game, or at least limit the time spent in the field the way you and your dog have been hunting since she was a pup. We either pretend that the dogs we hunt and live with will never age, never be capable of any thing but flawless performance or we refuse to admit that they are only here for a fleeting moment in our lives. It won't happen to *my* dog. Time is constant and there is no escaping its relentless passing. It is important that we take every opportunity to make this less than perfect time as good as it can be for the dog who has given so much of itself to us.

Like any other dogs, Anneca and Beth were not immune to the passage of time. Beth was in her twelfth season when her time came.

Over Thanksgiving weekend 1990 Anneca, Beth and I went to the cabin on a Ruffed grouse hunt. It would turn out to be Beth's last. I took the long way to the cabin thinking we could try our luck on chukar and pheasant at the Mercury Mine sixty miles from home. The past two seasons I had noticed that toward sunset, Beth had been running into things, as if she was having trouble in the fading light. She bloodied her nose running into a hog wire fence on a quail hunt on the Boise River and several times I had difficulty getting her attention to change her direction with hand signals. Four years earlier, after she was anesthetized so cheat grass could be removed from he ear, she lost her hearing. Deafness would be a major stumbling block for some dogs, but she took it all in stride. Although physically fit, her deafness, coupled with her failing eye sight, ment special considerations were necessary while in the field.

Bells were a necessity, no matter how open the cover was. It was also important to have a bell with a different pitch than Anneca's to be aware of Beth's location at all times and, if possible, have Beth in sight as well. Having control of Anneca was a big help because they hunted well together and usually kept each other in check. Even with all these precautions, there were some tense moments when I either couldn't get Beth's attention, or I'd lose sight of her and end up searching for her frantically .

The cover at the Mercury Mine is essentially wide open with mostly rocky outcroppings and sage. Several access roads bisect the sage and rocks, leading to different elevations of the surrounding hillsides. We arrived at first light, made the west side of the mine's access road, and hunted the rubble from the mining excavation at the base of the road first. Both Anneca and Beth were a little keyed up from the long drive and it took some reprimanding and a few stern looks before they calmed down. We left the main road and were working an abandoned portion of the original service road. Beth was on the downhill side, Anneca was uphill. We had traveled some three hundred yards when Anneca started getting birdy and slowed to a crawl, her head searching in every direction for the scent of game, her tail wagging in circles in anticipation of what was sure to unfold.

I had lost sight of Beth and could not hear her bell as Anneca locked up solid on point. There was no time to look for Beth and I moved in for the flush. A group of ten chukar exploded just downhill from Anneca and flew straight away from me and headed down the access road. I picked the outside bird on the left and squeezed the trigger, folding it clean. I quickly picked out a second bird and as

I fired, I saw Beth break into view some seventy yards down the road. It was too late to stop anything. I heard a yelp, then prepared myself for the worst and searched for a sign that Beth was alright.

To my surprise, she came trotting back as if nothing had happened. But as she drew closer, I spotted a small spot of blood on her right front leg. I pulled out my first aid kit, cleaned off the wound with water from the canteen and inspected the damage. She had a single number eight just under the skin. I was able to remove it with a slight pressure of my finger and thumb. I found another on the top of her right hindquarter and removed it the same way. My heart was racing. Thoughts of what could have happened sent me to the ground shaking holding on to Beth tight, begging her forgiveness. But with her, forgiveness wasn't necessary. She gave me a look that told me she understood; it was just an accident and it would be all right. We sat there, the three of us, looking to the valley below, thankful all was well with our world. Considering what had just unfolded, I decided to cut our lossed and head back to the main road and on to the cabin.

When we reached the bottom of the canyon, where the road crosses the Weiser River, I stopped the truck near a spot we had hunted several years earlier. There was an old cottonwood tree, half dead from the water backed up from a beaver dam blocking a small creek entering the river. Cattails lined the pond near the road's edge. Beyond, tall grasses held ideal cover for pheasants and duck that frequent the grain fields in the distant rich farm lands. Back in October of '86, Anneca and Beth had pointed, of all things, a large drake mallard at this very spot during a hunt at the Mercury Mine for chukar.

I was thinking back at how surprised I was at the sight of a duck jumping up from one of Beth's points when I spotted a fox hunting along the fence line at the far end of the dam. He moved another ten yards, looked in my direction, then disappeared into the tall grass near the cottonwood tree. No sooner had he disappeared from sight, when five rooster pheasants flushed from the base of the tree and scattered in all directions. One rooster flew directly at the truck and over the hood, then landed at the base of a dropoff near a set of railroad tracks. Two flew tight against the shoulder of the hillside, then landed in a patch of grass and willows at the edge of the river on the far side. The other two headed for parts unknown.

I wanted no part of this area. Nothing would have pleased me more than to see the river and the cottonwood dam shrinking in the rear view mirror, but the girls had seen the roosters, too. Their excited prancing and incessant whining, convinced me to stay.

Two birds in the brush are worth more than one by the tracks, so I decided to hunt the river's edge first. Backtracking to an access gate I saw on the way in, the only entrance to the river on that side, I planned our assault only to find a "no hunting" sign tacked to the gate. On to plan 'B.' I had made a mental note of where the first pheasant had landed. We walked down the road from the truck hoping to loop around the bird and pin him between us and the river. I expected he'd be on the run, but I was caught off guard when I reached the top of the hill and the bird flushed from under my feet. It was a straight away shot, but I missed with both barrels. Anneca and Beth, never doubting my shooting ability, took off in pursuit just as a train was coming down the tracks in our direction.

I looked down the railroad tracks and saw Beth and Anneca searching for the bird on both sides, crossing back and forth on the tracks as the train drew near. I called out, but the train was making so much noise. Anneca couldn't hear me and Beth was too preoccupied to see me jumping up and down, waving my arms like a madman. As the train drew nearer, the conductor saw Anneca and Beth on the tracks and gave several blasts on the whistle. Anneca heard the train and started toward me, but Beth was still searching for the bird, oblivious to anything but finding the rooster. The train was almost on top of her when she finally looked up and spotted it. Then, at the last minute, she stepped out from in front of the train and stood cowering at the side of the tracks as the train rushed by her, the wind from the front engine blowing the feathers of hair on her legs and tail like a dust devil blows bits of paper and dust.

Someone was trying to tell me something and I took their advice. We headed for the cabin hoping to leave behind the bad luck that had plagued us from the start.

The drive was longer than I had anticipated and it was dark by the time we reached the turnoff to the cabin. I brought along a large Blue grouse shot during this year's bow season for elk. I had roasted it the night before, so I just needed to reheat it on the stove. After dinner, with a roaring fire, a cold bottle of beer and Anneca and Beth by my side, I put the day's unhappy events behind me and planned for tomorrow's hunt.

Anneca and Beth were still curled up next to the glowing coals of the dinner fire from the night before when I came into the living room the next morning. I let them lie in sweet sleep while I made lunch and prepared breakfast -- pancakes, juice and a large diet Coke. The smell of breakfast woke my slumbering hounds and both ate their share of pancakes. After breakfast, I loaded up gear and headed down a back road to the east side of the lake. Earlier in the fall I had spotted several grouse at the side of the road in this area. Although there was a good foot of snow on the ground this morning, I was sure there would be luck for us today. I pulled into a spot where, earlier in the year, I had flushed a brace of grouse. As I stepped from the truck, I found fresh grouse tracks in the snow. They were heading uphill. I let Anneca and Beth out of the truck and cast them both in the direction where the grouse had gone.

Snow was stacked two inches high on every branch of cover as we headed up the draw. Every movement caused the stacked snow to cascade to the ground and down my neck as well. Anneca and Beth were working well and we traveled deep into the draw as the grade got steeper, and the snow grew deeper with every step. As we reached a second plateau, the ground started getting rocky and the walking became more treacherous. In light of yesterday's luck, I left nothing to chance and moved down back to the truck.

We drove on for a while, looking for an area that held the right combination of cover, water, and feed, when I spotted another group of tracks and pulled over to investigate. It was late morning and the tracks looked fresh. Once again they headed uphill. With noon approaching, I decided to make this the last hunt before lunch. The girls were excited and it took no coaxing to get them on line with the tracks.

The ground was flat for the first one hundred yards and was laced with roads that led only into another road. The checkerboard pattern of the surrounding trees and roads was perfect cover. I was sure we would find the grouse who made the footprints in the snow. Despite what seemed like ideal conditions, Anneca and Beth worked for twenty minutes without one productive. Reaching the base of the slope, we ran into several groups of tracks and two pairs of wing prints in the snow at the edge of a stand of fir. All were heading to the top, so we followed suit.

The first few yards were easy climbing, but further up the slope we ran into rocky ledges and I fell more than once along the way. When we made the top, I discovered we were on a ridge that overlooked a small basin that was totally hidden from the main road. There were a series of beaver dams that stairstepped through the creek, almost hidden by the snow. Standing there, our hearts still pounding from the climb, I spotted movement from the corner of my eye. It was a small herd of mule deer who wanted no part of the dogs or me and put as much distance between us as possible.

In the early fall, whenever we see deer while elk hunting, nine times out of ten, we run into grouse. Hoping the luck of the early elk season had some carryover, I followed in the direction of the deer. Their tracks cut a deep channel through the snow, making the trip down to the creek and beaver ponds easy. Soon we were hunting the stands of fir and willow in the basin below. There were grouse tracks along the edge of the creek and throughout the willows, indicating that the birds were feeding on buds. We traveled from one patch of willow to the next, always just one step behind the feeding birds.

Anneca and Beth had covered two hundred yards through the beaver dam basin when they suddenly became birdy, making short tacks through the snow as they searched the air for scent. I moved in behind the two and followed them into a group of fir trees. The trees opened up into a small park. As Beth entered, she slammed to a stop, causing a cloud of powder to rise up like a skier would when making a quick turn. A brace of ruffed grouse flushed simultaneously and headed for the opposite side of the park. I managed to get off a quick shot and dropped one of the grouse at the center of the opening.

The girls were on top of the grouse in an instant. Beth reached the bird first and was letting Anneca have no part of this grouse - it was her bird. I moved in quickly and grabbed the grouse from Beth before things got ugly. I held the bird over their heads while they both stuffed their noses deep into the breast feathers, their tails almost wagging off their bodies.

Their interest in this dead bird was short lived. They both turned to follow the line of flight of the second grouse and as I moved after them, I heard another grouse flush far ahead. Beth was on the slope above the firs, working a fire trail. Anneca was ahead of me when I lost sight of Beth. Anneca flash pointed at the base of a fir and as she rounded the tree, she bumped three grouse. I took a shot at the last bird but was well behind; the shot showed a pattern in the snow on the branches of one of the firs.

Calling Anneca back, I then noticed that Beth was nowhere in sight. Anneca and I sat on a log and listened for Beth's Bell. I could hear it every so often and made attempts to follow but when I got to where I thought it should be, I would hear it again in the opposite direction. I was starting to worry. With Beth's poor eyesight and total loss of hearing, it would be next to impossible to get her attention. Then I came across her tracks. They were heading back in the direction of the truck. With any luck, I thought, she would be there waiting when we returned.

We arrived at the truck in thirty minutes but Beth was nowhere in sight. I drove the road back towards the cabin in hopes of spotting her, but had no luck. Several times I spotted her tracks in the snow, but they always led back to the forest.

After four or five times up and down a three mile stretch of road, I spotted a family out fishing at a portion of the road where Beth's tracks had crossed. I stopped and talked to the father and asked if he had seen a dog running down the road in the past hour. He said a dog that matched Beth's description had run past them about a half hour earlier. He told me the dog was very keyed up and when it saw him, it ran back down the road then up into the trees. I thanked him for his help and gave him the cabin phone number with instructions to call if he spotted her again.

As I returned to my first parking spot where we had climbed over the ridge, I left Anneca in the back of the truck and climbed to the top of the ridge again. Once there, I sat on the edge looking down into the beaver dam basin hoping to spot Beth. An hour had gone by and my hopes dwindled with each passing minute as I watched the basin. Daylight was fading and so was my hope of ever finding Beth in this vast expanse. I was getting cold and hungry and I could hear Anneca barking back at the truck. I decided to drive the eight miles back to the cabin, change my clothes, eat and then come back in full control of my faculties.

Leaving the ridge was one of the hardest things I've ever done. I felt I had let Beth down and had given her up as lost forever. But deep down inside I knew this was the smart thing to do. Driving back I was shaking uncontrollably. The heater was taking forever to come on line, but finally kicked in just as I pulled into the cabin.

I was soaked to the bone. I Quickly started a fire, changed out of my wet clothes and hung them off the mantel to dry while I made a quick dinner. Anneca curled up next to the hearth while I cooked a pot of deer chili. Steam rose from her wet fur as she rested. Visions of Beth stumbling through the forest, bumping into trees and rocks with her poor eyesight and curled up shivering against an old tree stump, kept haunting me as I tried to collect my thoughts on how to find her. I managed to choke down a bowl of chili and quickly put on dry clothes. I checked my boots, but the bottoms of the insides were still wet. I put on an extra pair of socks and called it good.

The drive back seemed to take forever and that empty feeling in the pit of my stomach kept gnawing at my very soul. I thought that if Beth was still in the area, she would be disoriented enough to stay in one spot and maybe do nothing but bark. It was pitch black when we reached the section of road near the beaver dam basin. The overcast sky covered what light the moon might have provided. Anneca was upset and was panting and whining so much I couldn't hear well enough in case Beth *was* barking. I had made two passes on the stretch of road with no luck. I decided to stop the truck and walk the road so I could hear either Beth's bell, or her barking. At first I took Anneca with me but she was more intent on finding Beth herself than helping me. Reluctantly, I took her back to the truck and went on alone.

While I was listening for Beth barking, I was also looking for any new tracks in the snow that might lead me to her. I would drive the truck ahead two hundred yards or so, shut the ignition off and leave the headlights on, search for tracks in the snow, then walk back to the truck and repeat the process over again. I had made two full passes up and down the road when I returned to the truck to move it ahead, I got nothing but a few turns of the engine, then nothing but tick, tick, tick from the ignition. My battery was dead.

Eight miles from the cabin, in the middle of the night, at the end of November, lost deaf dog somewhere up in the mountains - things were not looking good. Just then, off in the distance, I heard what at first sounded like a chain saw. I stopped and held my breath so I could hear it more clearly and concluded it wasn't a saw after all, but rather a group of snowmobiles. I took Anneca by the collar and trotted down the road in the direction of the noise hoping there were trucks to haul the snowmobiles.

Sound carries well in the winter and it was two miles before we met up with the group. I explained my situation and they were more than happy to lend me a hand. Anneca and I rode in the back of the pickup. After our two mile run, we welcomed the rest. It took two tries to get the truck to turn over, but once it was running, I made sure the lights were off for awhile as we continued the search for Beth in the night.

I thanked them for their help and waited for the pickup to disappear around the bend before slowly driving the road again. As I made the second pass down the beaver dam stretch of road, I thought I had heard someone yelling. I was hardly running the truck above idle, with my head hanging out the window, when I heard the first yell. I stopped the truck, walked far enough ahead to muffle the engine noise and listened once more for the voices in the dark. Then I heard it again. Straining my ears and holding my breath, I listened to pinpoint it's location. Then I discovered it wasn't yelling I was hearing, it was barking! But I still couldn't locate the where it was coming from. The basin I was standing in made the sounds bounce off from one side of the canyon to the other, making it all but impossible to get a fix on Beth's bark.

I made another two passes up and down the road, listening, moving ahead, then listening once more as we slowly made our way down the road, before I decided to take a chance and check out the original entry we made into the beaver dam basin. Shutting the truck off, I stepped quickly out into the foot deep snow at the base of a crossing where a mountain creek cascaded from the beaver dam basin and passed beneath the road. Beth's barks were close, but the sound of the water made it difficult to determine her exact location. The climb was one of relief and worry. I was glad it was over but the grade of the climb was steep and the chance that Beth would get my scent and stumble into the falls had me concerned.

Her barking was nonstop. I used it like a homing beacon as I climbed higher. I was within five yards of her when I reached the top. Climbing over a rocky ledge and spotting her beside the trunk of a large fir, I realized she had no idea I was there. She sat and barked until I touched her side, then she jerked, surprised I had finally found her. Then she whined with excitement of being found.

The sound of the water from Beth's perch was deafening. The thought of her stumbling over the falls made my heart sink. I carried her down to the truck and somehow made it down without falling. Beth sat in the passenger side seat and we talked — even though I knew she couldn't hear me babbling. All was good again.

Back at the cabin, the coals from the dinner fire were still glowing in the fireplace sending off friendly shadows in the dim light. I wrapped Beth up in a towel, sat her next tothe hearth and added wood to the fire to warm us all.

This was Beth and Anneca's last grouse hunt. We spent

their remaining years hunting chukar and pheasant and as their muzzles began to gray, we switched to only pheasants. Beth and Anneca have been gone for more than three years now, but I still see them in my sleep, in the pages of my gun diary and in the photographs on my office wall. I am constantly catching my self looking out the back porch, half expecting to see them both, whitewashed against the cool grass in the shade of the box elder tree they spent so much of their last years enjoying. I was lucky; their *when* didn't come for twelve years and even after that, they still hunted into their fourteenth season.

The question often comes to mind if I could endure another *when*, another empty feeling of loss when the hunting companion I've hunted with for years only lives in memories and dreams. The answer is always the same. Yes. I'm a better man for knowing them. They've made my life more complete and as painful as it can be, I can't imagine my life without bird dogs. As I finish this last chapter, sitting with Briar, our seven month old English Setter, who has several points on grouse and pheasants already under his belt and just coming into his own, I can't imagine him ever having a when...

and so it goes.

Briar with the Author's son ~
Matt's first grouse.

Hidden deep within the tangle of tall grass and branches lie the quarry. Searching the air for the elusive scent of the game, stiff legged with head held high, the dog of white and brown stands motionless as her master approaches. She acknowledges his presence with a slow glance then quickly regains her stance in preparation for the events to come. Suddenly the whir of wings breaks the silence as a molted brown rocket explodes toward the safety of the dense pines above; gold and amber leaves trailing behind it.

As the echo of the gun's report fades across the canyon, she finds the bird. It is warm and holds the sweet bouquet that makes her soul burn. Quickly she picks the bird up, holding it gently between her teeth, and carrying it back, sits at her masters feet.

He takes the bird from her mouth to admire its beauty before placing it in the game pouch, while she sits at his side with a silly grin as if reflecting on a job well done.

The pause is broken with two pats on her head and "Good girl! Now let's find another!".